Learning to Read, Step by Step!

Ready to Read   Preschool–Kindergarten
• big type and easy words • rhyme and rhythm • picture clues
For children who know the alphabet and are eager to
begin reading.

Reading with Help   Preschool–Grade 1
• basic vocabulary • short sentences • simple stories
For children who recognize familiar words and sound out
new words with help.

Reading on Your Own   Grades 1–3
• engaging characters • easy-to-follow plots • popular topics
For children who are ready to read on their own.

Reading Paragraphs   Grades 2–3
• challenging vocabulary • short paragraphs • exciting stories
For newly independent readers who read simple sentences
with confidence.

Ready for Chapters   Grades 2–4
• chapters • longer paragraphs • full-color art
For children who want to take the plunge into chapter books
but still like colorful pictures.

STEP INTO READING® is designed to give every child a successful
reading experience. The grade levels are only guides; children will progress
through the steps at their own speed, developing confidence in their reading.

Remember, a lifetime love of reading starts with a single step!

*This book is dedicated to
all the big people who are
helping smaller people
learn to read.
The StoryBots love you!*

Designed by Greg Mako

All rights reserved. Published in the United States by Random House Children's Books, a division of Penguin Random House LLC, 1745 Broadway, New York, NY 10019, and in Canada by Penguin Random House Canada Limited, Toronto.

Step into Reading, Random House, and the Random House colophon are registered trademarks of Penguin Random House LLC.

StoryBots, Netflix, and all related titles, logos, and characters are trademarks of Netflix, Inc.

Visit us on the Web!
StepIntoReading.com
rhcbooks.com

Educators and librarians, for a variety of teaching tools, visit us at RHTeachersLibrarians.com

ISBN 978-0-593-30475-4 (trade) — ISBN 978-0-593-30476-1 (lib. bdg.) —
ISBN 978-0-593-30477-8 (ebook)

Printed in the United States of America

10 9 8 7 6 5 4 3

STORYBOTS

VELOCIRAPTORS

by Scott Emmons

illustrated by Nikolas Ilic

Random House 🏠 New York

On a visit
to the past,
we see

dinosaurs running

free and fast.

We stop to get
a closer view.

Velociraptors

coming through!

When those
scary beasts
appear,

it's time to hurry
out of here!

Just look at how
they scurry past.

They may be small,

but they are FAST!

That mouth is like
a mighty trap.

It closes

with a noisy SNAP!

SNAP!

Velociraptors
hatch from eggs.

They have sharp claws

and very strong legs.

They may have feathers,
but they cannot fly.

They learn
a hard lesson
if they try!

Their teeth are sharp
for chomping snacks.

At dinnertime,
they hunt in packs.

Meat is what
they love to eat.

For them, a rose
is not a treat!

If a raptor
chases you,
then you know
just what to do.

Wearing flowers
is the key
to staying safe
and raptor-free!

Goodbye, velociraptors!